Prepare to fly with your Star Dr

For all the children about to go on an exciting adventure...

Welcome to the star dragon book collection, a series of 6 different meditation story books featuring the star dragons and their friends. They are for you and your child to read together, and they are wildly imaginative.

This book is designed to calm children's minds before sleep and is a perfect bedtime adventure.

The star dragons live on the Draco star constellation, situated in the far northern sky, above the North Pole.

The story allows you to invite the star dragons down from their stars, so we can go on an imaginative journey with them and their friends to distant magical places.

The dragon's and their friends are here to help protect your child from nightmares and bad dreams by taking them off on a journey using imagination and breathing techniques. By using both imagination and breathing techniques before sleep will begin the process of calming your child's mind and settling them from stressed to relaxed. This allows your child to process stress and any uncomfortable emotions in their sleep and wake up feeling happier and calmer.

We call the dragons down from the stars using our breathing techniques throughout the book....

Let us begin.....

Please email nickyjp@hotmail.com to receive an MP3 audio that accompanies this book.

Visit www.coolkidswithcoolminds.org.uk for other products in the star dragon range.

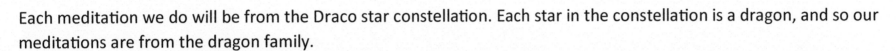

Each meditation we do will be from the Draco star constellation. Each star in the constellation is a dragon, and so our meditations are from the dragon family.

Purple Star Dragon is called Rastaban and Eltanin. They come from the star constellation known as Draco, in the far northern sky which wraps around the North Pole. Draco is Latin for dragon, and the stars represent the dragons, that once guarded the Gardens of Hesperides.

Rastaban and Eltanin are the dragon's eyes in the night sky, in the Draco star constellation. When the stars come down to earth, they change into a double-headed, purple dragon to guide you in your life.

So, we are going to call them down from their star. Then we can go off on a meditation with them.

Get yourself nice and comfortable, and close your eyes. Take a deep breath in and imagine blowing out purple breath. As you do, imagine sending purple roots out of the bottom of your feet, twisting, and spiralling all the way down to the centre of the earth.

As you relax and breathe deeper, imagine a beautiful, purple light shining down on the top of your head, all the way down through your chest, into your tummy, down your legs and out through your feet, until you see it glow deep in the centre of the earth.

As you relax, Rastaban and Eltanin, the double headed purple star dragon, floats down to the earth from the stars.

As they do, they turn from beautiful, bright stars into a beautiful, bright purple, double-headed dragon, that lights up the whole of your room.

As you climb on the back of Rastaban and Eltanin, their huge wings begin to slowly move up and down, and you begin to climb high into the night sky.

You feel the cool breeze on your face as you leave through your bedroom window.

The other stars in the night sky are shining brightly, and the stars in the Draco constellation are waving down at you, knowing you are going on an amazing journey with Rastaban and Eltanin.

As you fly high through the clouds passing the bright moon in the sky, a colony of bats pass you.

They have come from the caves that Rastaban and Eltanin are taking you to.

They are off to sit with children sleeping in their beds to protect and keep them safe from any nightmares they may have. As you keep flying higher and higher, and further into the night sky you realise you have flown behind the moon.

You are now in total darkness apart from the purple glow of Rastaban and Eltanin, the double-headed purple star dragon.

Keep blowing out your purple breath as you ride on the back of Rastaban and Eltanin.

In the distance you begin to see a small light shining. You are not sure what this is, but as you fly closer and closer to it, it becomes bigger and brighter.

Eventually you get so close the light becomes so bright it almost blinds you.

Rastaban and Eltanin appear to be flying down towards the bright light, and you begin to see the mouth of a huge cave. This is the home of the bat colony you passed earlier, as you were flying behind the moon.

As you get nearer and nearer to the caves, the bats are circling around, and one flies down to join you.

His name is Alcathoe.

"Hello," he says. "Where are you from?"

"I am from earth," you reply.

"Why are you here?" Alcathoe asks in a puzzled voice.

"I called Rastaban and Eltanin down from the stars with my purple breathing," you reply.

"Wow! That's pretty cool," replies Alcathoe, "welcome to our world" he says.

"Where are we?" you ask.

"We are far, far up in the night sky but at the same time, we are deep below the sea," replies Alcathoe, the bat.

"How can that be?" you ask.

"The two places are allowed to exist together. When the star dragon's come down to visit, they help us look after the children at night and protect them from nightmares."

As you begin to get closer, you enter the mouth of the cave and hear beautiful, soft singing. All the bats and the dragons are singing together, and this makes the cave very happy. It light's up all the crystals in the cave with pure joy and happiness, and they begin to sing too.

As Rastaban and Eltanin sit down on the floor of the cave, you jump off their back and begin to walk around. The crystals are all singing softly and clearly, and they glisten and vibrate as the bats and dragon's sing in harmony. This begins to make you feel very calm and relaxed.

Keep blowing out your purple breath as you listen to the soothing music coming from the singing crystal caves.

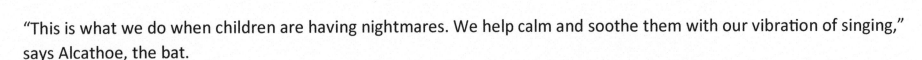

"This is what we do when children are having nightmares. We help calm and soothe them with our vibration of singing," says Alcathoe, the bat.

"It gently relaxes, and calms children's minds and makes them forget all the worries they may have that can bring on nightmares. Once they are all back asleep, we keep singing gently until morning. Then we return to our bat caves where we go to sleep. And the dragons return to their stars so they can sleep too. Then, every night, we return to help the children again," explains Alcathoe.

Rastaban, Eltanin, and Alcathoe, the bat, have enjoyed being in the singing crystal caves with you, and they would love for you to return anytime you like.

The vibrating singing crystals are making you very drowsy, so you climb on the back of your purple double-headed dragon Rastaban and Eltanin. You set off flying high out of the caves and out into the night sky. And at the same time, you rise high out of the sea, as you fly back around the bright huge moon. As you do, you see the bats returning home to their caves, and you safely return to the comfort of your own bed.

"Was I having a nightmare?" you ask.

"Yes," Rastaban and Eltanin reply.

"Therefore, we brought you to our special singing crystal caves so that you could hear all of us singing. So, when you fall asleep, if you begin to think of us, the crystal cave, and our singing, you will feel safe, relaxed, and protected. Then you can go to bed and sleep peacefully," says Rastaban and Eltanin reassuringly.

Lie in bed listening to the beautiful sound the crystal caves are making and practice your purple breathing and Alcathoe and Rastaban and Eltanin.

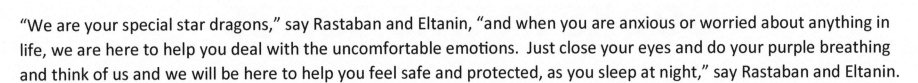

"We are your special star dragons," say Rastaban and Eltanin, "and when you are anxious or worried about anything in life, we are here to help you deal with the uncomfortable emotions. Just close your eyes and do your purple breathing and think of us and we will be here to help you feel safe and protected, as you sleep at night," say Rastaban and Eltanin.

As quick as a flash Rastaban and Eltanin have flown back up to the Draco star constellation in the night sky, to shine with all the other star dragons. As you look out of your window it makes you feel happy to know the stars are looking down on you too.

When you open your eyes why not draw what you saw in your meditation? And also, a picture of yourself blowing out your purple breath!

Books in this series

Blue Star Dragon and the Golden Grids
:
Green Star Dragon and the Centre of the Earth

Red Star Dragon and Atlantis

Silver Star Dragon and the Silver Forest

Yellow Star Dragon and the South Pole

Purple Star Dragon and the Singing Crystal Caves

Also available in poster form

Visit: www.coolkidswithcoolminds.org.uk

Write you Dragon story here...

Draw your own Dragon here..

Draw what you saw in your meditation here...

About the Author

Nicola Parkinson is an Osteopath, Meditation teacher and Neurodevelopmental Therapist.

I have been meditating for over 30 years and wanted children to experience the peace and calm that meditation brings.

The Star Dragon Collection was born in lockdown 2020. When I was not working for the first 3 months, I had time to focus on my children's work, thinking how I can incorporate a meditation for children to enjoy and gain the same benefits from it that I did.

I have always had a liking for Dragons and to bring the Star Dragons to life was an absolute pleasure, and so exciting as it began to unfold.

The stories wrote themselves when I was deep in meditation.

I truly hope you enjoy them as much as I do, and enjoy their friends whilst on the adventures with the dragons.

The name of each dragon is a star in the Draco Star constellation, and the names of their friends are an actual breed of the species of animal. Please google them to see!

I wanted children to be enchanted and also educated then they can understand we need to treasure and look after mother nature and her friends.

Watch out for more to come from Star Dragon Meditation Stories.

In the ever-increasing stress of lives, children are struggling to cope more and more

In the environments considered normal today,

stress is increasing and affecting our children's academic, physical and mental health.

And the pressure to help them is falling more and more onto parents and carers to help them cope.

The Star Dragon books are a tool for emotional wellbeing as they introduce a child to story time with

breathing techniques and an MP3 audio, that helps

their minds to calm down, unwind and begin releasing stress.

Using breathing techniques with imagination and an audio with brainwave music helps your child to:

- Release anxiety
- Increase wellbeing
- Stimulate concentration, focus and absorption of information
- Release uncomfortable emotions
- Process emotions better
- Help them to use breathing techniques regularly to help them cope.

www.coolkidswithcoolminds.org.uk

FB: Star Dragon Meditation Story Posters